PRINCESS PEARL

FALKIRK COUNCIL
LIBRARY SUPPORT
FOR SCHOOLS

For Pearl, with love – G.A.

For Dilly – S.W.

ORCHARD BOOKS

96 Leonard Street, London EC2A 4XD

Hachette Children's Books

Level 17/207 Kent Street, Sydney NSW 2000

ISBN 1 84362 310 2

First published in Great Britain in 2005

A CIP catalogue record for this book is available from the British Library.

10 9 8 7 6 5 4 3 2 1

Printed in China

PRINCESS PEARL

Giles Andreae

Sophy Williams

ORCHARD BOOKS

T here was once a young princess whose name was Pearl. Her mother and father were the King and Queen of the Ocean, and Pearl lived with them in a wonderful palace beneath the sea. Its walls were built of flaming orange coral, the colour of sunsets. Its roof was decorated with sparkling blue shells and the floors were covered with carpets of woven emerald seaweed as dazzling as the jewels themselves.

Everyone who came to the palace was
overwhelmed by its splendour and its
beauty. Everyone, that is, except for Pearl.
Because Pearl was unable to see.

Pearl had been blind since she was born. She found her way around the many rooms and corridors of the palace by touching the walls, by feeling the furniture, and by the sounds of things – how they echoed and resonated.

But there was another way in which Pearl was guided through her strange, dark world as well. A young servant boy had been allotted to her ever since she could walk, and it was he who, in time, became Pearl's eyes. His name was Charis, and he came from the islands above the water.

Every time she bumped into something that had been
left in her way, or put something down and forgot where
to find it, Pearl would turn to Charis.

"Where's my hairbrush, Charis?" she would shout in
frustration, or, "My dress! I can't find my dress!"

Charis would always calm her down with gentle words
and they would often end up laughing about it together.

But as Pearl grew older, and she became used to the feel of every step and every corner of the palace, she began to ask Charis what it was like above the water on the islands where he used to live.

"My Princess," Charis would always reply, "your palace is below the sea. It is a magnificent place. It is the wish of your parents that you should remain here and learn all you can about this kingdom, for there will come a time when it will all be yours."

But Pearl could hear the yearning in Charis's voice and one day, when they were out swimming together between the rocks, Pearl reached out for Charis's hand. She held it tight and kicked as hard as she could towards the surface.

Before long, their heads broke through the water and Pearl, for the first time in her life, felt the warm sun on her face.

"Where are we, Charis?" she laughed.

"This is my island!" said Charis. "This is the island where I was born!" He looked around and felt a warm rush of love for the place that had once been his home.

He took Pearl's hand and led her up the beach.

"Oh, Pearl," he said, picking a flower from a tree at the edge of the sand.

"What is it?" asked Pearl, leaning forward.

"Frangipani."

"It sounds as beautiful as it smells," said Pearl.

"Feel it," said Charis.

Pearl took the flower in her hands. The petals were soft and waxy between her fingers. Charis fastened it into her hair and Pearl ran down the beach until the warm water was lapping around her ankles.

"Come on!" she said to Charis. "We'd better get back before my parents notice we're missing!"

So Charis took her hand and together they swam back towards the underwater palace.

Pearl put the flower in a little box she had made from shells, and locked it in a drawer of her dressing table. And, from that day on, every time she felt bold enough, Pearl would lead Charis up to the surface of the ocean and, together, they would explore every treasure that the islands had to offer.

Charis picked ripe peaches for Pearl to taste. He took her to spots where the birds sang more sweetly than anywhere else on earth. And every time she would return with a little flower, a leaf or some blossom, all of which she locked into the small shell box in her bedroom.

These moments all found their
way deep into Charis's soul. At times
he was so full of love for Pearl that
he felt like his heart would fly. And
both of them thought that these
precious days would last forever.

But the days turned to months and the months turned to years, and it wasn't long before Pearl had become a beautiful young woman.

One morning, the King and the Queen summoned Pearl to their chamber and sat her down.

"Pearl," said her mother, "your father and I have decided that it is time for you to marry. As is the tradition in this kingdom, we have already chosen the two most suitable husbands for you.

"Prince Maravick's family is not wealthy, but he is nobly born, and he is one of the bravest warriors in the kingdom.

"Prince Araman," she continued, "is, as you know, the son of a great friend of your father's. His kingdom stretches from where the sun rises to where it sets and he has riches that most men can only dream of.

"They are both coming to the palace a year from today. Whichever man you choose will be your husband."

"But Mother!" began Pearl.

The Queen raised her hand.

"The wedding will be set for the following day," she continued. "We will have a feast and a celebration in the Great Hall, the likes of which this kingdom has never seen before!" And she swept out of the room.

Charis led Pearl back to her bedchamber in silence.

"Oh Charis, what shall I do?" she said. "I don't know either of these men at all. Can I not choose a husband for myself? And besides," she added, "I am not ready to be married."

Charis hung his head and held Pearl's hand a bit more tightly. "I know, my Princess," he said, "I know," and a tear fell from his eye. Pearl could not see the tear, but she could hear it in his voice.

That year was the saddest year of Pearl's life. The marriage felt like a great weight around her neck.

Her trips to the surface of the ocean with Charis became more infrequent and then stopped altogether. How could she enjoy her few glimpses of freedom when she felt like she was already a prisoner?

When the day finally arrived, Charis helped Pearl to prepare herself.

She put on her cloak and walked slowly into the Great Hall.

She sat down on her princess's throne. Her parents had invited many members of the court to witness the event.

"Prince Maravick the Mighty," announced the King, and the Prince stepped forward.

"Princess Pearl," he began, "I am sure that you will choose me to be your husband. I may not have the riches of Prince Araman but I am the bravest warrior this kingdom has ever known and, so I am told," he continued, "the most handsome."

His voice oozed like honey, but honey that you had just had too much of, and left you feeling sick.

"What do I need a husband who is handsome for," replied Pearl, "when I am unable to see? And why do I need a husband who is brave when I already have a whole army to protect me?"

Pearl's mother coughed loudly. Prince Maravick returned to his place.

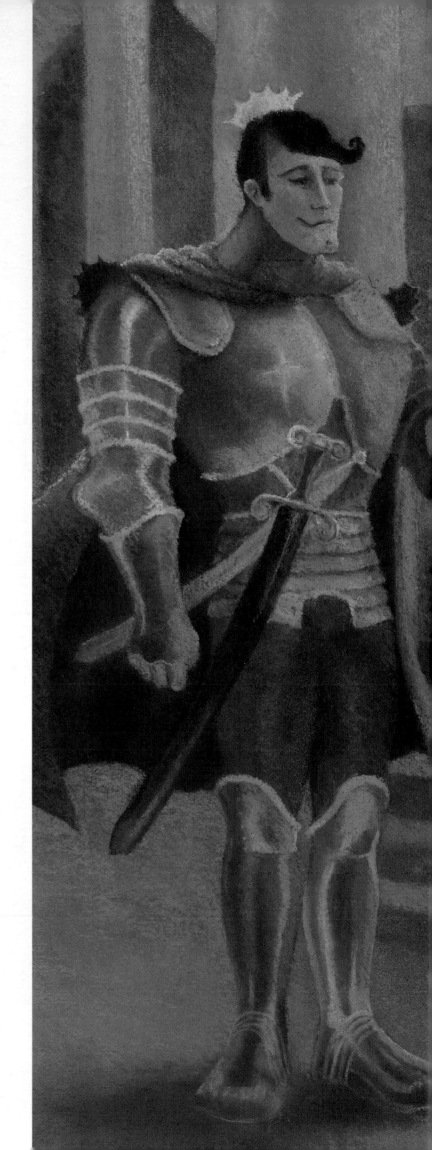

"Prince Araman of the Islands," the King then announced.

Prince Araman stepped forward. He summoned two of his servants who, between them, were carrying an enormous chest. They laid the chest at Pearl's feet and Prince Araman opened the lid. The courtiers gasped at what they saw.

"Princess," he said, "if you marry me, all this treasure, and much, much more will be yours." His voice was sharp and spiky like the jagged rocks which Charis had so often led her around on their adventures outside the palace walls.

Pearl stepped down from her throne and passed her hands over the treasure. She picked up golden goblets, necklaces encrusted with jewels and diamond-studded bracelets.

"What use is this to me?" she said. "These may be the most beautiful things to you, but to me, what I am holding feels hard, cold and lifeless."

"Just like all of you," she wanted to add, but thought better of it.

"Pearl, really!" said her mother, stepping forward. "You must choose one of these fine men." She smiled over-generously to each of the Princes as if to make up for her daughter's rudeness.

"I have chosen my prince, Mother," said Pearl.

"Thank goodness," replied her mother. "Which one shall it be?"

The King, the Queen, the Princes and the courtiers waited eagerly in silence for her reply.

Then she spoke.

"Charis," said Pearl softly.

"Charis?" snorted her mother. "You can't possibly marry Charis. Don't be ridiculous. He's a servant boy!" At that, many of the assembled courtiers began to laugh.

Pearl stood up and stepped down from her throne.

"I may be blind, Mother," continued Pearl, "but there is one thing that I can see and it's the most beautiful thing in the world."

"Oh yes," said her mother, "and what may I ask is that?"

"His heart," replied Pearl softly.

"Me?" said Charis, stepping forward in disbelief. "Pearl, you love me?"

Pearl took out the little shell box which she had hidden beneath her cloak. Charis saw that all the flowers had been perfectly preserved and they shone now like beautiful coloured jewels.

"With all my heart," she said.

Charis's heart welled up with love, with pride and with a joy stronger than anything he thought it was possible to feel.

He took Pearl in his arms, closed his eyes, and held her tightly. Then, to the astonishment of the whole court, Charis lifted Pearl lightly off her feet and walked out of the Great Hall towards the palace gates.

Outside, in the warm ocean,
Charis took Pearl by the hand and,
together, they swam off towards the
surface, with their faces stretched
out to the sun.